Sea Foam and Blood

AMY LAURENS

OTHER WORKS

SANCTUARY SERIES

Where Shadows Rise
Through Roads Between
When Worlds Collide

KADITEOS SERIES

How Not To Acquire A Castle
Define Good
How Not To Ring The Hero's Bell (2020)

STORM FOXES SERIES

A Fox Of Storms and Starlight

SHORTER WORKS

Dreaming Of Forests
Darkness and Good
Of Sea Foam and Blood

NON-FICTION

How To Write Dogs
How To Theme
How To Create Cultures
How To Create Life
How To Map
The 32 Worst Mistakes People Make About Dogs

Find other works by the author at
www.amylaurens.com

Sea Foam and Blood

INKLET #29

AMY LAURENS

www.inkprintpress.com

Print ISBN: 978-1-925825-28-2
eBook ISBN: 9781393811664

www.inkprintpress.com

National Library of Australia Cataloguing-in-Publication Data
Laurens, Amy 1985 –
Sea Foam and Blood
58 p.
ISBN: 978-1-925825-28-2
Inkprint Press, Canberra, Australia
1. Young Adult Fiction—Fantasy—Contemporary 2.
Young Adult Fiction—Animals—Horses 3. Young Adult
Fiction—Health & Daily Living—Diseases, Illness &
Injuries 4. Young Adult Fiction—Short Stories

First Print Edition: March 2020
Cover image © Joan Greenman via Pixabay
Cover design © Inkprint Press
Interior art © Amy Laurens

SEA FOAM AND BLOOD

Adelaide laughed as Anchor cleared the jump with room to spare. She lined him up for the final obstacle.

Her side twinged.

She clenched her teeth and ignored it. Just one more jump. She rocked back and forth in time with Anchor's smooth canter, and her side caught again. She sucked her breath in sharply.

Adelaide aimed Anchor straight at the jump, judged the take-off and tapped him gently with her heel. He flew over the jump.

Adelaide didn't.

From the pathway up to the house, her mother screamed.

How typical of Mum to appear now. Adelaide groaned and sat up, winded but otherwise fine. She grabbed the jump and hauled herself to her feet.

"Stop!" her mother called. "Lie back down right now!"

Adelaide rolled her eyes but did as she was told. She lay down and breathed in the grassy smell of the paddock. The evening dew was settling and the air smelled fresh and clean. Almost as good as—horse.

She grinned as a noseful of warm horsey air announced Anchor's arrival. He snuffed her face, tickling her with his whiskers and nickering.

Inhaling the comforting smell of horse sweat and partially-digested grains, Adelaide raised a hand to his cheek. "Hey, gorgeous. What's doing?"

Satisfied that she was all right, Anchor raised his head. His ears flicked as he watched her mother approach.

Adelaide sighed as he backed away. This wasn't the first time she'd felt caught between the two of them. Their peace with each other had been uneasy since the day Anchor had arrived.

Her mother knelt by her side. "Are you okay, sweetheart?"

"Mum, I'm fine."

"Do you hurt here? What about here?"

Adelaide tried to sit up, but her mother's insistent hands held her down. "Mum, honest, I'm fine."

"How many fingers?"

"Two hundred."

"Funny. Any blurriness of vision? Head pain? Dizziness? Blacking out?"

"No, no, no and additionally, no. I'm fine!"

Her mother pursed her lips, but rocked back on her heels. "Are you sure?"

"Yes!" Adelaide tried not to roll her eyes.

"One of these days you'll be thankful for my caution, Miss Adelaide Kelton," said her mother, halfway between teasing and tears.

Adelaide tried to look innocent, and sat up. Her side twinged again and she flinched.

"Ah ha!" Concern lines deepened on her mother's forehead. "I knew you weren't fine."

"Mum, it's nothing." Adelaide scrambled to her feet and stepped towards Anchor.

"Oh no you don't. You'll not be going near that beast again."

This time Adelaide did roll her eyes and, impatient with her mother's theatrics, walked towards her horse.

"No."

Anchor shied at Mum's harsh tone.

Adelaide turned, ready to glare at her. But the strange look on her mother's face froze her. "What?"

"I mean it, Adelaide." Mum folded her arms. "This time enough's enough. I've already spoken to your father. You'll not be riding anymore."

Adelaide's pulse raced. What kind of cruel joke was this? She shook her head in disbelief. "But, Mum—"

"No buts. I'm sorry. You won't be riding him again."

Adelaide fought the tears welling up in her eyes and the anger growing in her chest. "Mum, this is completely unfair! It was just one tiny fall! I'm fine!"

"No, Adelaide, you're not. And I won't have you out here risking your life any more. Sooner or later you're going to have to accept—"

"I have accepted it, Mum! But just because I'm going to die doesn't mean

I need to curl up and do it now! You're the one who hasn't accepted it. You try to wrap me up in cotton wool as though that will somehow make me live longer! It won't, Mum. I'm going to die."

Her mother jerked back as though slapped, her face pale.

Adelaide's temper abated and she cringed. That had been a bit low. But before she could apologise, her mother spoke.

"Get inside. Now."

Adelaide bit her lip and headed for the house.

That night, Adelaide dreamed again. It was the same dream she'd had for weeks now, and she knew it well.

It began on a beach as the waves caressed the shore, leaving wet kisses on the sand. The light of a full moon traced a silver path across the ocean as the air brought salt to her nose, the taste of it sharp on her lips. Adelaide smiled.

A whicker.

She turned to the bronze-coloured horse and her smile broadened. "Hey, boy. It's good to see you again."

She held up a hand and the horse pressed his nose into it, huffing. She stepped closer and he rubbed his head against her, nearly knocking her over. Adelaide giggled. "Steady, boy."

She ran her hands through his coppery mane and frowned. The colour reminded her of something, but she couldn't remember what.

She shrugged it off and stepped to his side. She took hold of his mane, flexed her knees, and jumped up onto his back.

Her stomach fluttered. She knew what would happen next, but a part of her couldn't help hoping that this time would be different.

"Don't fall." A voice drifted across the beach with the breeze and Adelaide's stomach knotted.

The horse reared and she leaned forward, gripping his mane in her fists and his sides with her legs.

But his coat was too sleek, and as always she found herself sliding over his rump, catching madly at his tail and sprawling in the sand as the magnificent horse raced off into the distance.

She lay on her back, winded, and stared up at the stars.

Blood, she remembered. His mane was the colour of blood.

Adelaide stumbled down the path, clutching at her father's arm. She'd woken the morning after her fall feeling fine, but not long after breakfast the twinge in her side had become pain, and shortly after that it had become a fire that consumed her whole left side and made it hard to breathe.

And so Doctor Rose had been called in for yet another examination. Everyone had known it was all just for show. There was nothing he, or anyone else, could do. But despite Adelaide's protests, Doctor Rose had sided with her parents: no more riding.

Adelaide had been crushed, but a tiny part of her she couldn't silence knew that they were right; now, a couple of weeks later, it was an effort just to get to the bathroom.

But today she'd convinced her father to walk her down to see Anchor, and as they neared the paddock with the scent of damp dirt filling the air and hay-dust from the shed tickling the back of her throat, she searched eagerly for any sign of her wonderful grey gelding. "Where is he, Dad? I can't see him."

"He'll be there," said Dad. "As soon as he sees you he'll come racing over, I guarantee it."

They halted at the paddock rails. Adelaide clung to them for support, shading her eyes against the sun. "I still can't see him, Dad."

"He must be in the bottom corner."

Adelaide nodded. "Can you get his feed pail?"

Dad left, and returned moments later with Anchor's metal feed bucket. Adelaide took it and began clanging it against the paddock rails. "Here, Anchor! Here, boy!"

A moment passed. Anchor appeared over the crest and Adelaide's face split into a grin.

"Here he comes," said Dad. "Galloping like a maniac, just like I said he would."

Adelaide giggled. He was a maniac that horse, more so than was good for him. Speed went straight to his head, and he never watched where he was putting his feet once he felt the wind in his nostrils.

Adelaide drank in his movement, fluid and precise as his muscles bunched and released, bunched and released.

He moved beautifully.

He stumbled.

Adelaide gasped in horror, but he continued galloping, and she relaxed.

But something wasn't right. His movement wasn't smooth anymore, and it soon became evident that one of his legs wasn't working properly.

"Slow down!" Adelaide waved her arms wildly and clambered through the railings. "Anchor, stop!"

A scant twenty metres from the fence he stumbled again and fell, crashing to the ground.

Adelaide screamed.

Anchor thrashed, but couldn't seem to get his feet under him.

"No! Anchor!" She raced over to him, ignoring the burning in her side and her father's shouts for her to stop, come back, slow down.

She reached Anchor and dropped to her knees near his chest. "Quiet boy, lie still." She shook her head at the desperation in her voice and tried again. "It's okay. Just lie still and we'll fix you right up." She laid a hand on his shoulder.

At her touch, he quieted. He snorted, trembling, but lay still.

"That's it, there's a boy." Her insides writhed as she realised that the bulge partway down his canon was bone, pressing out against the skin.

Dad crouched next to her. "Is he all right?"

Adelaide shook her head and ran her hand up his leg, stopping just below the break. She watched with fascinated horror as a trickle of blood met her fingers.

Dad regarded the scene for a moment, then placed a hand on her shoulder. "Adelaide, come up to the house and we can call the vet. Please."

She stared up at him and he flinched at the strength of her gaze. "I'm not going anywhere."

He nodded. "I'll go call the vet."

She crawled around to Anchor's face, ignoring the stabs of pain from her side, and cradled his head in her lap. Right now, his pain was more important. She stroked his cheek. "You'll be fine. Shh now."

Anchor grunted and tossed his head, flaxen mane spilling over his eyes and into Adelaide's lap.

"Shh," said Adelaide, grasping his head and pressing it back down. "Stay still, there's a good boy."

His big, liquid eye blinked up at her, and he snuffed at her knee.

Adelaide tried to smile and realised that tears were streaming down her cheeks. She sheltered his head with her body. "I love you, boy. It'll all be okay." She broke off with a sob. Unwittingly, her gaze ran down his body towards his leg. She sobbed again and gripped Anchor's head in a tight hug.

"No," she whispered. "Please no. Not you too."

Her father returned after a short eternity, followed by the vet, Dr Cathson. "You were lucky," Dad said. "She was in the area."

Dr Cathson nodded to Adelaide and placed her bag on the ground next to them. She knelt by Anchor's chest and ran her hands down his leg, going slowly over the break, examining it, probing it, while Anchor trembled and winced.

Adelaide held her breath and clutched Anchor's head. "There's a boy," she crooned. "Just lie still."

The vet finished her examination.

Adelaide saw her shoulders tense as she nodded at Dad.

Adelaide glanced back and forth between them. "What, what is it?"

"Adelaide." Dad crouched beside her and took her under the arms. "It's time to go inside."

Adelaide's chest contracted. "No!"

He lifted her to her feet and began to walk her away from her horse.

"No!" she screamed, desperately trying to break free of his grip. "No, let me stay! I want to stay with my horse!"

"Adelaide, come on. We have to go."

"No!" Tears streamed down her cheeks. Her body convulsed as she sobbed. "Please, please Daddy, no!"

But he kept walking, implacable, dragging Adelaide away as the vet injected the fat vial of lurid green poison into Anchor's neck.

Adelaide's eyes fluttered open and for a moment she could still feel the sand beneath her. The dream had grown more vivid with each night that passed. Sometimes she wasn't quite sure if this wasn't the dream. Perhaps she was only awake when she was on the beach.

She sighed, the burning in her side reminding her that, dream or not, this was her reality for now, and it wasn't a pleasant one.

The week since Anchor's death had passed in one long blur. Mostly Adelaide had lain in bed, flipping through photos of her with various horses, lingering over the ones that showed her with Anchor.

She'd ridden other horses before him. She'd even had other horses stay on their property. But Anchor was the first she'd been able to call hers. No-one else's, just hers.

And now he was gone.

The tiny, rational part of her knew it didn't matter. Doctor Rose had given his last prognosis—one month, maybe two—and she could feel that he was right.

But the rest of her—the large, emotive, creative, imaginative part, the part she felt was her in all her essence—that part knew it wasn't fair.

To take Anchor away from her like that, when she had so little time left anyway... that was just cruel. She hadn't even been able to hold a service for him, as she had for every pet she'd ever owned.

Her gaze fell on her model horses, standing haphazardly on the shelf above her desk. She smiled at her ceramic Pegasus, given to her by Aunt Lizzie years and years ago. The body was blood bay, and the wings a bright brassy gold.

Adelaide had always thought they ought to have been green, like the sea from which Pegasus had been born.

Pegasus, born of sea foam and the blood of a dead monster.

She turned back to her photos. The one on top was one of her favourites—Anchor and herself cantering bareback down the beach.

A thought struck her and she raised herself up on her elbows. Yes, she thought. Anchor would have liked that. He'd always loved the sea.

She glanced out the window. Full moon. It would be perfect.

There was a tap on the door, and Mum poked her head into the room. "How are you?"

Adelaide licked her lips nervously. It drained her strength even to walk between rooms, these days, and her plan would probably kill her. It wasn't like she particularly cared—but her parents might.

"Mum," she said breathily. "Can you sit down for a moment?"

Her mother sat on the bed and took Adelaide's hand. "What is it?"

"Mum, there's… there's something I have to do."

The colour left her mother's face, and her jaw twitched, just once. "Yes?"

"I want to take Anchor's ashes down to the sea." Adelaide's stomach flipped, but she held her mother's gaze. "Please."

For a long moment there was silence as Adelaide's mother stared at her. "Will you make it?"

Adelaide felt a flood of relief. She hadn't offered to drive, which meant that at least in some small way she understood.

Then Adelaide realised what Mum had asked. "I… I'm not sure."

Tears brightened her mother's eyes. "When will you go?"

"Tonight."

A tear spilled over. "Oh, Adelaide." She reached forward and scooped Adelaide to her. "How am I going to live without you?"

Adelaide's throat constricted and she hugged her mother fiercely. "It'll be okay, Mum. You just have to keep going. One day at a time."

Adelaide eased the back door shut, breathing heavily and trying hard to ignore the pain. The urn containing Anchor's ashes weighed down her backpack like it was solid gold.

The walk to the beach, only a few hundred paces to the edge of their property, seemed to take forever. Adelaide stopped every few steps to regain her breath and hunch down in her jacket, glad of its warmth in the cold night air.

The moon was close to setting when she finally found herself on the sand. As she looked out over the waves, her breath caught in her throat.

It looked just like her dream.

She took off her shoes and slowly, haltingly, she shuffled down to the water's edge. The sand was cold, but it scratched pleasantly at her feet and she closed her eyes, listening to the sound of her steps: gentle squeaks in the fine, dry sand, dull thuds as the sand grew firm, and then squelches in the water-logged sand near the waves as the gentle breeze waved the scent of salt water around her.

A rush of water over Adelaide's toes made her jolt her eyes open. It was cold, and thick with sea foam.

She shivered a little and hugged herself.

For a moment she stood staring out into the distance. The moon's reflection was a silver trail extending all the way to the horizon.

Adelaide imagined what it might be like to walk that path, following it to the moon.

The waves shushed about her ankles and she remembered her purpose. She unslung her backpack and drew out the urn. A tear trickled down her cheek. "Goodbye, Anchor."

She threw the urn as hard as she could so the ash flew out. It dropped into the ocean a little way away, right at the beginning of the moon path.

Adelaide smiled through her tears. "Goodbye."

A breeze whipped in from the sea and Adelaide shivered. She'd done what she'd come to do; it was time to go.

She waded out of the water. As she reached the dry sand line she tilted her head, listening.

Was that a whicker?

She must be imagining things. Grief did that to people, she'd heard. She shook her head and stepped forward.

Another whicker.

Throat tight, Adelaide turned.

Right in front of her, salty water still streaming off him, a large, bronze horse was emerging from the sea.

Adelaide blinked.

The horse paused in the shallows to shake himself violently, sending spray flying like silvery glitter in the moonlight. He pranced the last few steps and stopped in front of her.

"Um, hi," said Adelaide, breath catching in her throat.

The horse tossed his head.

Adelaide held up her hand, and the bronze horse pressed his nose into it. Not quite sure if she was awake or dreaming, Adelaide giggled.

The horse stepped closer and rubbed his head up and down against her.

"Careful," she said. "You'll knock me over!"

He tossed his head again, and his mane whipped against Adelaide's face.

His mane. His *blood*-coloured mane. Adelaide gasped, eyes wide.

The horse whickered again and bobbed his head impatiently. Adelaide shivered. She was supposed to mount now, but fear froze her and she clutched at the big horse's head.

Then her side twinged and she decided. Maybe she would fall, maybe she wouldn't, but she was not going to die without trying.

She moved to the horse's side, grabbed a fistful of mane and jumped, hauling herself onto the horse's sleek, bronze back. She grinned. She was on.

"Don't fall." The voice from her dream drifted through her head. Adrenalin rushed through her body. What would happen if she couldn't stay on? Would it kill her if she fell?

A strange pulsing motion caught her attention and she looked down. Adelaide gasped. Huge frothy wings unfurled behind her knees, transparent, shimmering and barely there.

Like sea foam.

Adelaide leaned forward and wrapped her hands in the horse's mane, laughing. With wings to brace her legs against, there was no way she would fall.

"Let's go!"

The horse leaped, bucking and kicking, and jumped into the air. They gained height with every wing beat and Adelaide gasped in sudden realisation. Not only was the ground falling away—the pain was too.

She pressed her forehead against the horse's withers and sucked in a deep breath of horsey air. "Thank you," she said. "Thank you."

The horse turned, and flew towards the moon.

THE MAKING OF *SEA FOAM AND BLOOD*

This, lovely reader, was the first story I ever, ever sold. And even then, we have to use the term 'sold' a bit loosely: it was to a non-paying market, now-defunct. I did end up getting paid for the story, though, as I had the privilege of winning the Readers' Choice award for the issue, which was terribly exciting!

Not-so-secret confession: I loved English in high school. A whole course where pretty much all you had to do was read and write? Sign me up now!

I got pretty good grades, too—except my last ever assignment, in Year 12, a creative piece. I decided to do a visual creative instead of writing a story, just for a change, and it was super fun, but I also had to write a rationale to go with it explaining my artistic choices, and for whatever reason—probably because it was my last ever assessment task for high school—I just did *not* write a decent rationale.

I didn't *fail* the assessment task, but it was close.

For a couple of years, even though I kept the artworks (because I'd invested a lot of time into them after all), I couldn't stand to look at them, because they only reminded me of how I'd screwed up that assignment.

Fast forward four years. I've finished my Bachelor's degree at university, with a couple of creative writing courses thrown in there. I'm active on Critique Circle, and slowly working on learning how to write short stories— and one day, I come across those old artworks in a box in the spare room.

They remind me of the mythology I'd been studying when I'd created the artwork: the story of Pegasus, born from the ocean when Medusa's blood sprayed over it as she died.

I've always loved horses; I've always been into mythology.

The story practically wrote itself.

And although these days I'm more sympathetic to poor Medusa, I'm even more into pegasi and unicorns and anything horsey and magical than I was as a kid—and my body's more broken than ever. Flying away on a magical Pegasus and leaving all physical pain behind? Yes please. That sounds great.

DOWNLOAD YOUR FREE EBOOK

When you buy a print book from Inkprint Press, we like to say THANK YOU by offering you the ebook for free!

Please head to www.inkprintpress.com/inklets/29/ and the use the coupon INKLET29 to get your copy of this Inklet in epub AND mobi today!
(Coupon will only work once.)

Read more by Amy Laurens!

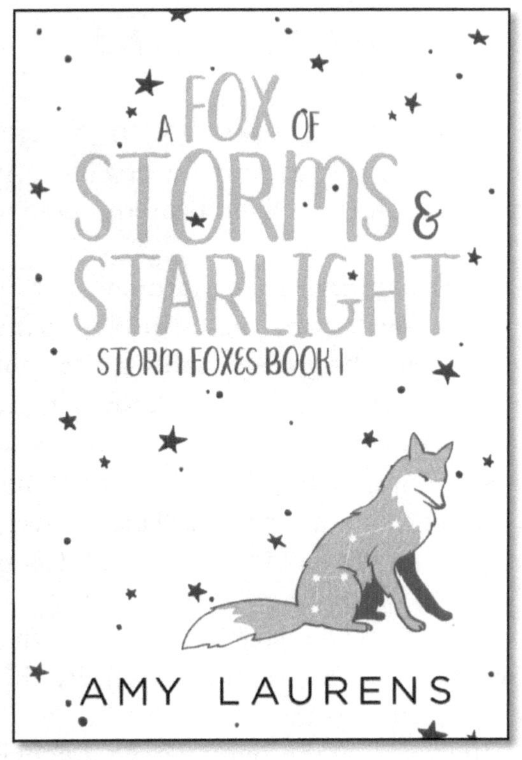

A FOX OF STORMS AND STARLIGHT

CHAPTER ONE

SIX YEARS AGO, I SAVED A FOX IN THE bush. It was only because my dog died. At the time, it felt like a pretty crappy bargain.

It was the first day of autumn—not by the calendar, but by the fresh bite in the morning air, the golden quality of the light as it lit the main road through town in the mid afternoon.

Sailor was a big, black shaggy thing, something like a Newfoundland, a lively shadow in the golden light, and I was eleven.

I'm sorry to be starting any story this way, but the fact of the matter is, this where it all began.

I'll spare you the awful details. Enough to say that Sailor had got out of the yard somehow, and had been hit by a truck careening down the highway that split our tiny town in two as it blatantly ignored the speed limit.

I saw it happen.

And although I cradled him in my lap as the smell of burnt-out brakes and hot asphalt and turning leaves filled my nose, his giant, furry black head all of him I could fit, there was nothing I could do.

There was nothing anyone could do.

I knew that, but it didn't stop the knot of frustration and guilt in my chest, or the taste of bile in the back of my throat every time I closed my eyes and saw the truck hitting him, again and again and again.

It took years for that vision to fade.

But that evening, only a few hours after it had happened, everything still felt fresh, and raw.

Sunny, my sister, was only nine at the time. She cried for hours, just sobbing like she'd never breathe right again.

I'd cried a little, at the scene with Sailor's head lying in my lap as his big, brown eye stared up at nothing.

It had been mercifully fast, there was that.

And the driver had copped a massive fine—speeding, reckless driving, I think they even defected his truck—and came to visit us later, a big, pot-bellied man standing on our front verandah, shuffling his royal blue cap round and round and round in his hands as he apologised.

But that evening, with Sunny sobbing her heart out on the couch in the living room and Mum and Dad trying desperately to console her as dinner burned on the stove, I couldn't cry, even though the acrid scent of burning soy sauce, scorching brown sugar and smoking rice wine from the marinade prickled the back of my throat and the corners of my eyes.

I was the eldest, and I had to be responsible.

Possibly, if I'd been just a little more responsible, Sailor wouldn't have died.

So I slipped out the glass slider from the family room to the deck while Sunny cried, glancing up at the two storeys of our moody grey house behind me before jumping heavily down the three steps from the rail-less deck to the lawn, and set out for the gate in the back fence.

I couldn't cry, and I didn't want to add anything to an already chaotic and stressful situation inside—but I couldn't stay there, either.

In the gaps between the gum trees to the west, the sky tinged to red and gold at the horizon, the sun sinking slowly into oblivion. I'm pretty sure I didn't know the word oblivion back then, but I knew what it meant, how it felt—and I craved it, desperately.

Anything would be better than the gaping hole in my chest.

And so, because I didn't know where to find it or how to get there, I stalked through the bush, pushing myself until I breathed hard and my lungs ached and sweat ringed me, chasing the way that hard exercise elevated me over my constantly looping thoughts.

Directly above, dark, heavy clouds obscured the sky, and the air was thick, heavy, humid.

Beneath the smell of dry gum leaves and even drier dirt, I could catch a hint of ozone, and occasionally the wind turned cool for a breath as it gusted against my skin, promising a late evening storm.

I walked harder, faster, outrunning the video looping in my mind of the truck's impact.

When the first drops of rain spat at me from out of the sky, I barely noticed. My skin was filmed with sweat, slick and salty, and the peppering of rainwater barely added to it.

That was at first.

But within minutes, it became clear that those first pattering spits had been the early foreshadowing of a storm darker and more intense than any I remembered.

Thunder rolled across the sky, distant and grumbling at first, a lazy background chorus to the rhythmic melody of the rain as it splattered down on grey-green leaves and red-tinged twigs, turning the silvered bark of an old, dead gum to deep grey and making the spiky, tussocky grass seem oddly luminescent in the dying light.

I stood under a grey gum with stains down its trunk that the rain was turning orange, arms wrapped around myself, shivering hard—and for the briefest instant, thought about not going home.

Mum and Dad would pitch a fit.

And I had to be responsible.

I turned, dark t-shirt plastered to my skin, dark hair sticking to my face and clinging to my neck, and began trudging my way back. The storm closed over properly, clouds rolling over the horizon and cutting off the thin scythe of blood-coloured sky, making the bush dark and unwelcoming in the premature night.

Lightning flashed.

Thunder cracked hot on its heels.

I jumped—and stared hard at the gap between two ghost-barked trees, where for a second, I was sure I'd seen a pair of eyes.

Nothing moved.

Nothing except the drenching rain, anyway, weighing down the branches that tossed fitfully in the wind.

The smell of wet dirt and soaked bark rose around me, undercut by eucalypt and ozone.

If anything had the power to wash away the hurt inside me, this storm was it. I tipped my face to the sky, imagining the rain washing over me had the ability to wash me inside as well, and the raindrops splattered hard on my face.

More lightning. More thunder, cracking over top of the constant hiss of the falling rain.

And in the distance, something eerie, lifting the hairs on the back of my neck: a strange kind of high-pitched howl, a cry that rang with moonlight and distance, cutting straight through the noise of the storm.

Bolts of lightning streaked across the sky—one—two—three in the space of half a second, followed immediately by a growling crack of thunder so immense it vibrated in my chest. I ducked instinctively.

There, in the corner of my eye…

I froze, crouched with my arms over my head.

The strange cries came again—and they were closer.

I stared hard at the place, low to the ground, where I was sure I'd seen something small, maybe the size of a cat.

Flash. Growl.

Rain spitting down.

There. Right there. A small animal, pointy ears, light coloured chin and throat...

The strange, eerie cries came a third time, and my heart pounded fiercely. Whatever was making the noise, it was close. Really close.

The little creature across from me reacted too, flattening itself to the ground.

My jaw twitched.

My heart pounded.

My fingertips bit into my upper arms.

Stay? Go?

Run? Freeze?

The hairs on my neck prickled again and goosebumps broke out all over me.

Cold dread formed a knot in my stomach.

Something was coming.

Something worse than the storm.

I had to get home.

I made it halfway to standing—and a series of strange, awful noises made me freeze again. They were sharp, clacking, squealing sounds, like someone knocking two echoing stones against each other, interspersed with high-pitched yowling...

And the creature in the darkness screamed.

I threw my back against the gumtree behind me, pressing hard against it. My heart hammered.

I peered back and forth in the dark, eyes wide.

Rain drenched down, but my throat was dry.

My pulse pounded faster.

The little creature screamed again—and as lightning flashed, I saw it on its back, legs slashing wildly at the air as something attacked.

The awful, clicking-yowling noises grew louder.

I slapped my hands over my ears, gasping. Water ran down my face, getting into my mouth, my eyes.

It was hurting.

Whatever the small thing was, it was getting hurt, and I'd seen enough animals hurting today.

Something in my chest snapped.

I flung myself across the ground, leaping a couple of tussocks and a fallen branch before I crashed to my knees.

I crawled closer, desperate, gasping for air through the heavy curtains of rain.

I couldn't see it. Where?

Somewhere here, near the base of that tree…

The yowling screeched right next to my ear. I cowered against the ground, spiky grass pricking my face, wet-earth smell smothering me—but now, there was a strange mustiness too, a cousin to wet-dog smell.

At the next flash of lightning, I saw it.

The creature was a fox—and something barely visible was attacking it, only the gleam of eye or flicker of teeth visible in the gloom.

But the damage was real enough.

The little fox's side had been opened right up, and in the bright, stark flashes of heavenly electricity, the blood was dark, thinned by the constant rain.

No.

No more animals were going to die today.

Not when this time, I could do something about it.

I snatched at a branch on the ground that turned out to be more of a twig, and launched myself toward the creature.

I had no idea what was attacking it, but I screamed and waved my handful of twiggy leaves anyway, batting them in the air over the fox like I knew what I was doing.

The horrible clacking cries ceased.

With one long, low rumble, the rain began to ebb.

Still gasping for air, pulse galloping in my throat, I sat next to the fox and shifted it carefully into my lap, realising as I tasted salt that I was crying.

I huddled over, trying to shelter the poor creature from the slackening rain, running my fingers over its wiry cheek— over and over and over and over.

"Please," I sobbed, throat tight and aching, chest constricted. "Please. Please don't die. Please."

Another gust of cool air washed over the clearing, taking the last of the rain with it—and lifting the goosebumps on my arms again.

I shivered, drawing the fox close, like it was a stuffed animal I could hug for comfort—its comfort or mine, I couldn't say.

"Please. Please don't die. Please."

Something shifted in my lap.

Around us, the world stilled, dazed from the storm, but also something more, something watching, something waiting, as the bush held its collective breath.

The only sound was the occasional drip of rainwater from the gum leaves onto a fallen log—no insects, no wind, no rustling of leaves. Just... stillness.

And the fox, who shivered in my lap.

The clouds tore open, revealing a ragged triangle of stars that glittered in the fox's eye as it blinked open and stared up at me.

My chest snagged.

My throat ached from crying, and a headache was forming in the back of my head. But the fox blinked up at me—alive.

I ran a finger down it again, from nose to cheek to ear to shoulder, all the way down its side to its thick, bushy tail—and the wound in its side began to close.

Laboriously, it hauled itself to its front legs.

I tried to stop it—"No, it's okay, you can stay here, I'll look after you"—but it lifted its top lip to show half-hearted teeth, and staggered away.

As it did, I thought perhaps its fur began to shrink. And suddenly, it looked larger in the night—as large as a dog, as large as Sailor…

But I blinked, and it was just a trick of the light, because the creature that darted away into the bushes like nothing was wrong at all was clearly a fox, the size of a large cat or maybe a small beagle, and nothing more.

And if something screamed in the night not long afterward, and the cry sounded horribly, horribly human?

Well. I was halfway back toward home again by then, and I pressed my fingertips to my lower eyelids and prayed my parents wouldn't murder me for getting home so late.

Keep reading! Head to www.amylaurens.com/ books/storm-foxes/ to buy your copy now!

ABOUT THE AUTHOR

AMY LAURENS is an Australian author of fantasy fiction for all ages. She's never flown on a Pegasus, but she did used to ride horses, and she has flown a plane a couple of times. Surely that combination counts, right?

Amy has also written the award-winning portal-fantasy *Sanctuary* series about Edge, a 13-year-old girl forced to move to a small country town because of witness protection (the first book is *Where Shadows Rise*), the humorous fantasy *Kaditeos* series, following Evil Overlord Mercury as she attempts to acquire a castle, the young adult *Storm Foxes* series about love and magic and mental health, and a whole host of non-fiction.

INKLET #031
Welcome to Dark Dale
LIANA BROOKS

INKLET #032
When War Came to Town
A Powers Story
AMY LAURENS

INKLET #033
Not Fantasy
AMY LAURENS

INKLET #034
Courting the Winter Prince
LIANA BROOKS

INKLET #035
At the Home of the Winter King
A Storm Foxes Story
AMY LAURENS

INKLET #036
With This Ring
AMY LAURENS

INKLET #037
Venus & Seven Reasons I Said No
LIANA BROOKS

INKLET #038
OATH KEEPER
AMY LAURENS

INKLET #039
FORGET
A Powers Story
AMY LAURENS

INKLET #043
NOT QUITE
Cinderella
LIANA BROOKS

INKLET #041
ONE BAD MAN
AMY LAURENS

DOUBLE ISSUE
INKLET #042
The Claustrophobia
Of Loneliness &
Adam, Be A Star
AMY LAURENS

INKLET #045
The Artist
as a Young Girl
LIANA BROOKS

INKLET #044
CONFESSIONS
AMY LAURENS

INKLET #046
But For Snow
A Kaiheos Story
AMY LAURENS

INKLET #049
The Boy
Named NO
LIANA BROOKS

INKLET #047
Anamata
AMY LAURENS

INKLET #048
A Wolf FOR
Christmas
AMY LAURENS

www.ingramcontent.com/pod-product-compliance
Lightning Source LLC
Chambersburg PA
CBHW031036190726
48286CB00003BA/1199